PICTURE CLASSICS

THE ADVENTURES OF ROBIN HOOD

Robin the Outlaw
Little John • The Silver Arrow

HISTORICAL SETTING

In 1066, Duke William of Normandy left France to invade England in a battle that came to be known as the Norman Conquest. Having succeeded in dividing the country, the Norman followers of William seized the Saxon land barons' property, and reduced the former noblemen to slave status.

England was still under Norman occupation when Richard the Lionheart became king in 1189. Shortly after his reign began, King Richard left England to help defend the Holy Land. Upon his departure, Richard appointed the Bishop of Ely temporary ruler. In a short time, however, the bishop's authority was usurped by Richard's evil brother, Prince John.

When informed of the turmoil in his kingdom, Richard began the journey home. Along the way, he was captured and jailed by the Holy Roman Emperor, Henry VI. No one knew King Richard's whereabouts, and few believed he would ever return alive. Thus, Prince John continued to wreak havoc on the king's helpless subjects.

ROBIN HOOD'S
OAK TREE

ST MARY'S
ABBEY

GISBORNE
CASTLE

WOODSTONE
CHURCH

In the twelfth century, when England was ruled
by Norman kings and their barons,
wandering minstrels began telling stories
of a great hero. He lived in Sherwood Forest
and, with his band of outlaws,
fought the Normans and protected
the Saxons. That hero was Robin Hood.
Stories about him are still told today – not just in
England, but all over the world.

Retold by John Grant
Illustrated by Victor G. Ambrus
Woodcuts by Jonathan Mercer

Cover illustration by James Bernardin

Originally published in the United Kingdom by
Ladybird Books Ltd © 1994

First American edition by Ladybird Books USA,
a division of Penguin Books USA Inc.
375 Hudson Street, New York, New York 10014

Printed in Great Britain
10 9 8 7 6 5 4 3 2 1

ISBN 0-7214-5652-9

CONTENTS

ROBIN THE OUTLAW

Early one summer morning, Robin of Locksley—a Saxon gentleman by birth and character—left his home at Locksley Hall and set out for the great and ancient forest of Sherwood.

The forest was a dark and dangerous place, where thieves and outlaws lay in wait to prey on unsuspecting travelers. Robin knew these woods and the ways of the people who lived there. So it was with caution that he proceeded to meet his friend, the fair Norman lady, Marian Fitzwalter. He was to escort her safely to her father's house.

Shouldering his longbow and quiver of arrows, Robin scanned the ground for any signs that might warn him of danger. At first, there were only a few scattered deer tracks in the dirt. But when he came to a broad path, he spotted a number of footprints and hoof marks. A sizable party had passed this way not long before. They appeared to be headed for the road on which Marian Fitzwalter and her party were traveling.

Frowning, Robin continued down the path. The travelers could not be far ahead, yet he heard no sound. Whatever their business, they were going about it very carefully, which made Robin uneasy.

Soon Robin came to a portion of the road that ran through a hollow. Now he could hear faint sounds of movement. Inching forward, he looked down into the hollow. Almost hidden among the bushes and the ferns was a group of armed men. He could just make out the shape of a horse and rider across the road.

It was an ambush—and Marian Fitzwalter was riding right into it!

I must stop her! thought Robin. Circling around, he reached the road just below the hollow. A moment later, Marian and her servants came into sight.

Robin shouted a warning, but in the same instant an armed horseman crashed through the bushes, blocking Marian's way. Marian's horse reared up in fright as armed men sprang out on all sides and stood in a semicircle across the road.

His bow at the ready, Robin called from the shadows, "Clear the way, Knight, and let the lady pass freely!"

"Who's there?" the knight shouted.

"I warned you!" Robin declared. The next moment the knight fell from the saddle with an arrow in his heart.

Robin leapt between Marian and her attackers. Finally, they recognized him. "Locksley! Saxon dog! Stand aside!" snarled a second knight, sword in hand.

The attackers closed in. Even at this close range, Robin was ready. He shot three more arrows, and three more Normans were slain.

Robin set another arrow in his bow, but the rest of the men fled. They dared not face Robin of Locksley, renowned as the most accurate bowman in Nottingham—if not all England!

Marian looked down at the dead knight. "Roger de Mortmain," she said. "One of my family's most bitter enemies!"

The attackers closed in.

"We must hurry now," said Robin. "More of de Mortmain's people may be looking for you. He had many evil supporters. The sooner we reach your father's house, the better." Taking the horse of the slain knight, Robin led Marian's party through the trees.

They rode at top speed, but it was midday before they came in sight of Malaset Manor, the home of the Fitzwalters. After Marian and her father greeted each other, Robin described what had happened.

"Robin of Locksley," said Sir Richard Fitzwalter, "you have done my family a great service. Roger de Mortmain was an evil man. No reward I could offer would be high enough. But you have put yourself in great danger. Killing a Knight of the Realm is a grave offense. The High Sheriff of Nottingham is bound to issue a warrant for your arrest. You must flee at once and go into hiding."

"No," replied Robin. "The sheriff, or his crony Guy of Gisborne, is more likely to take revenge on me by attacking my people. I must return to Locksley without delay!" And he set off at once for home.

As Robin neared the edge of the woods and the open fields, he heard a rustle in the undergrowth. A voice called softly, "Master! Master Locksley! Over here!"

Robin knew the voice. It was Will Scarlett, a poacher by trade and no friend to the royal foresters. He was dusty and disheveled, with blood on his face from a wound on his cheek.

"You must go no further," Scarlett said. "Gisborne's men are lying in wait for you. They claim you have committed a terrible crime; they have laid waste to Locksley."

"What of my people?" asked Robin anxiously.

"They had some warning," said Will. "The families escaped to nearby villages. But some of the men were taken prisoner."

"Gisborne trusts that I will come to their rescue," said Robin. "I won't disappoint him."

They hurried to Locksley Hall. Robin shook his

"That's far enough, Saxon!"

head as they looked upon what remained of his home. Smoke still rose from the ruins. Stables, cottages, and barns had been leveled. The mill smoldered darkly in the distance.

"Mutch the miller's son was captured," Will reported. "Gilbert the ditcher and Nic the carter, too."

"How many of Gisborne's men are still there?" asked Robin. "How are they armed?"

"Six stayed behind with the prisoners, armed with swords only," replied Will.

Robin thought for a moment. "Here's what you must do, Will," he said, and whispered his instructions.

Will nodded, picked up his bow, and slipped away through the trees.

Robin strode across the open ground to the rubble-strewn courtyard of the ruined hall.

"That's far enough, Saxon!"

A sergeant and two armed men stepped out from behind a burning gable.

15

Robin glimpsed three more men, partly hidden by a wall. All six, he thought. Good. The prisoners may be bound, but they are unguarded. Perhaps they are close by…

"Ah, Sergeant!" he called. "Had I known you were visiting, I would have stayed to welcome you to my humble home."

"Home?" laughed the sergeant. "You call a murdering Saxon's rat's nest a home?"

"Serving in Gisborne Castle," replied Robin, "you must know all about rats' nests!"

"Enough talk, Robin of Locksley!" shouted the sergeant. "You are under arrest for the heinous crime of murder."

"And who will arrest you?" retorted Robin. "There has long been a law against burning people's houses…"

"Seize him!" cried the sergeant.

Gisborne's men ran forward. Robin advanced to meet them, sword in hand. One went down after a thrust through his sword arm. A second reeled back, dazed from the smack of the flat of Robin's blade across his neck.

At the sergeant's command, the three remaining men rushed into the fight. Smoke swirled through the air as Robin fought off their attack. He was a good swordsman and battled bravely, but he was outnumbered. Where was Will Scarlett?

Suddenly one of the soldiers screamed and fell, transfixed by an arrow in his side. Will with his bow and four other men throwing stones and pieces of wood charged across the courtyard and joined the struggle.

"I have a good Saxon arrow for the last man to drop his sword!" shouted Will.

But before anyone could move, Mutch cried, "Back!" and pulled Robin by the sleeve. The Saxons scrambled clear just as the fire-weakened gable of Locksley Hall crashed to the ground. The sergeant and his men vanished under a heap of broken stone in a cloud of smoke and ash.

From the edge of the forest, Robin looked back at his ruined property. "I have nothing now," he said to the men around him, "except my sword and my longbow. Locksley is no more. I am Robin the outlaw and must take my opportunities where I find them."

"We are all outlaws," said Will Scarlett, "including Hal, here. He brought us warning."

The man nodded. "Hal the fletcher," he said. "I was delivering arrows to the Gisborne garrison when I heard the orders being given. I came as quickly as I could." Hal grinned. "I stole one of Gisborne's horses to speed my way."

Mutch laughed. "Here am I, a miller without a mill, and now an outlaw. My companions? A murderer, a poacher, and a horse thief. A merry company indeed!"

Led by Will Scarlett, the small band entered Sherwood Forest. As a poacher, Will knew every secret path and hidden glade. The sun was setting when he finally called a halt. They were in a wide clearing. A stream flowed nearby. A high rock to one side stood

The small band entered Sherwood Forest.

like a watchtower. "I suggest we camp here tonight," said Will.

Nic lit a fire. Will went off with his bow and returned shortly with the carcass of a young stag. "Tonight we dine on royal venison," he cried, "as served at the table of our true King…Richard the Lionheart."

"And of his evil brother, John," said Gilbert.

"But not in such fine company," laughed Mutch.

Using their hats, they all fetched water from the stream—all, that is, except Robin.

"I have no hat," he said, "only the hood of my jacket."

Mutch laughed again. "Then I would be honored to share mine with you, Robin o' the Hood!"

"Yes!" cried Will Scarlett. "Robin of Locksley is dead. Long live our leader, Robin o' the Hood!"

LITTLE JOHN

Robin called the men together.

Shortened to "Robin Hood," Mutch's nickname for Robin of Locksley stuck. The band of outlaws grew quickly. Some were men of Locksley, like Will Stutely. Others were tradesmen, like Arthur Bland, a tanner from Nottingham. He was outlawed because he had beaten a Norman merchant who had cheated him in business.

One day, Robin called the men together. "There are almost forty of us now," he said. "We are all wanted men. So we must be ready to fight for our freedom. We also must fight to defend the poor, the weak, and the helpless."

"But how can we fight?" asked Nic. "None of us are warriors, and we have no weapons."

"Then you must learn," said Robin, holding up a stout pole. "First you will learn how to fight with quarterstaves. We have a champion in our midst—right, Mutch?"

"I did win a prize at Nottingham Fair," Mutch confessed, blushing, "but that was only for sport."

23

"Not the way *you* play!" laughed Hal the fletcher. "You left ten opponents with very sore heads."

"Right," said Robin. "I appoint Mutch our quarterstaff instructor. Each man will cut an ash staff for himself. Then somehow we must find swords, bows, and arrows. We will be a small army, but to keep order we must have rules," he went on. "First: Greed and cruelty are our enemies."

"And Normans," said Will Stutely.

"Not all Normans," Robin pointed out. "We can count on several important Normans as friends. The Fitzwalters of Malaset, for instance. Saxons can be cruel and greedy, too. All who travel through Sherwood Forest should be invited to contribute money or goods to help the weak and helpless. And if they don't like the invitation, then they will be, let's say, 'persuaded,'" said Robin, with a sly grin.

"I see!" cried Mutch. "We shall rob the rich to feed the poor! And, as we are poor, we shall also feed ourselves. Very simple, really."

Robin continued. "Peasants, farmers, squires, knights, pilgrims, and beggars may pass freely, except those whom we know to be villains or troublemakers."

Day and night, the outlaws took turns keeping watch from the high rock. One morning there was a shout from the lookout.

"Something or someone is moving along the Nottingham road!" he called. "The birds and wild animals are very disturbed. It may be a company of many!"

"Dick!" Robin called to one of the young outlaws. "Keep out of sight and find out who is taking the high road to Nottingham."

Within an hour, Dick was back. "It's a covered ox cart," he reported, "with an armed guard of eight soldiers—four riding in front, and four behind."

"Supplies for the castle," said Robin. "I think we

might change that to supplies for Robin Hood and his men!"

The slow-moving cart and its escort stopped in a clearing where the road forked. A poor man's hut stood by the roadside.

"Peasant!" bellowed the captain of the escort. "Which is the road to Nottingham?"

There was no reply. The captain dismounted, strode over to the hut, and banged hard on the door. At the same moment, an arrow thudded into the wood, a hair's breadth from his fist. The captain whirled around. A second arrow hit the door on his other side, close to his shoulder. The captain drew his sword and started to shout an order. But a third arrow grazed the top of his helmet, then struck the door above his head.

"*I* shall give the orders!" called a voice from among the trees. "You are surrounded. And we have more arrows than you have soldiers!"

There was a stirring in the trees. The soldiers could make out the half-hidden figures of men behind the

The captain drew his sword.

trees and bushes. The Normans knew they were outnumbered many times over.

The mysterious voice gave the orders quickly. The Normans obeyed, dismounting and dropping their swords to the ground. Looking fearfully about them, they crowded into the dark, windowless hut. Then someone closed the door and barred it from outside.

Only then did Robin and the outlaws come out into the open and uncover the cart. It was loaded with long, wooden crates.

Hal opened the first one. "Arrows!" he exclaimed. "And bows!" There were also swords and sword-belts—all destined for Nottingham Castle.

The outlaws emptied the cart. Two to a crate, they headed back to the camp.

Will Scarlett and Robin collected the weapons dropped by the Normans. "I believe in telling the truth," laughed Robin. "We did have more arrows than they had soldiers. It's just a good thing that they didn't know we had only two bows!"

He crossed to the peasant's hut. "Robin Hood thanks the Sheriff of Nottingham for his generosity," he called to his Norman prisoners. "Long before you manage to break free, we shall be far away. We leave you your cart and horses. It is a long walk from here to Nottingham, and in any case animals and prisoners are too much trouble for us to feed and guard. Good-bye, and safe journey to you all!"

The High Sheriff of Nottingham raged when the news reached him. Prince John was even more furious. "Robin Hood! Robin Hood! That's all I hear!" he shouted. "Even my own stable boys and servants speak of no one else!"

By training and practicing every day, the outlaws became quick and accurate with their new weapons. Before long, few could equal their skill at quarterstaff, swordplay, and archery.

Soon, greedy landlords and harsh Norman overseers

were being stopped on forest roads and "persuaded" to hand over their riches. Then money, food, and clothing began to appear mysteriously at the doors of cottages in poor country villages.

Many of these country people lived and worked on lands owned by the Church. These peasants were required to pay rent to live on this land. When a few greedy Church men raised the rent, Robin and his men ambushed the rent collectors and recovered the peasants' money.

One day, after a successful raid, the outlaws were journeying homeward. The path they were following opened into a broad meadow divided by a wide, deep stream. A fallen tree bridged the waterway.

As usual when crossing open ground, the outlaws were very cautious. Robin went first, hurrying toward the log bridge. He was just turning to signal the others, when he heard a loud shout from the far bank.

A tall, burly man stood with one foot on the fallen tree. "One moment, friend!" he cried. "I want to cross!"

"By all means!" Robin called back. "As soon as I've come over, the way will be free for you to cross."

"No, no!" shouted the tall man. "I have right of way, as I have already set foot on the bridge. Step aside like a good fellow." And he laughed and twirled a long staff in front of him.

Robin unslung his bow. "I do not yield to threats!" he said angrily.

"Then let us dispute it man to man!" declared the other. "But I am unarmed except for my staff. Bow against quarterstaff is hardly fair." He laughed again and thumped the end of the staff on the tree trunk.

Robin laid his bow and quiver on the ground. "Lend me your quarterstaff, Nic," he called. The outlaws came out into the open, and Nic tossed Robin his ash staff.

The two men advanced to the middle of the log. Robin's opponent gave a great laugh. "Now, archer, let's see you really fight!"

The forest echoed with the crack of staves.

Robin used all his skill, but he could not land a single blow. Neither could his opponent, although he was a head taller and had a longer reach than Robin. They were a match for each other.

The forest echoed with the crack of staves as each man swung and parried. Then Robin slipped and lost his balance. With a resounding splash, he tumbled into the water.

The big man peered into the stream, where Robin's staff floated among the ripples. Robin was nowhere to be seen.

"I hope I haven't drowned your friend," the big man called to the outlaws. "I rather liked him—"

His voice broke off as Robin, who had surfaced on the other side of the log, grabbed his ankle. The tall man splashed into the water. A moment later, the two stood up and waded, laughing, to the bank.

Robin pointed to the bridge. "The road is clear," he said. "You may continue on your way now."

"In a moment," the man chuckled, "after I get my

breath and empty my boots of water."

The outlaws crossed to join them. Nic asked the man, "Where are you bound?"

"To find my cousin," said the big man. "I heard he was in these parts. Wanted by the law. Trouble with a cheating Norman leather merchant. Arthur Bland, they call him. Perhaps you've heard of him?"

Robin and the outlaws roared with laughter. "Heard of him? He's one of our company!" said Robin.

"Then you must be Robin Hood!" exclaimed the big man, joining in the laughter. "I'm John Little, until recently a cattleman on a farm near Mansfield. I'm in much the same sort of trouble as my cousin—a Norman steward got in the way of my fist! You're not recruiting by any chance, are you, Master Hood?"

"Well," grinned Robin, "we do happen to have room for a fellow like yourself. You may join us on one condition. We are a merry band and fond of a joke. You will forget that you were ever John Little. From this day, you will be known as Little John. Agreed?"

Robin and the outlaws roared with laughter.

"Agreed," said the man. "Little John I shall be—in name, if not in size or deed!"

Little John became a popular member of the band. None could be down at heart in his company, and he was a strong and fearless fighter. In time, he would become Robin Hood's right-hand man.

THE SILVER ARROW

One of Robin Hood's trusted friends was a monk named Brother Anselm. Robin once asked him, "Why not join us here in the forest? Like our king, Richard the Lionheart, we are God-fearing Christians. We need a chaplain."

Brother Anselm replied, "No, Robin, my work is with the sick in the Abbey infirmary. However, if you want a man of peace to serve your band, seek Brother Tuck of Copmanhurst. He has upset the abbot of St. Mary's because he refuses to accept a fee for marrying people. What's more, the monk usually brings a haunch of venison to the wedding feast, so he is also an enemy of the royal foresters. And," added Brother Anselm, "instead of 'Brother,' he refers to himself by the French title 'Friar'—Friar Tuck."

A few days later, Robin, with Little John and half a dozen others, set off to find Friar Tuck. Near the edge of Copmanhurst Forest, they came to a stream. There, holding a fishing line, was a burly man with a shaved head and dressed in a monk's habit.

Robin approached him. "Holy man," he said,
"I wish to cross the stream. Will you, like good Saint
Christopher, carry me?"

"As you wish," said the monk, leaning over so
Robin could climb on his back. He waded into the
stream and quickly reached the far bank. "Now,"
said Robin, "I would be obliged if you would take me
back again."

Without a word of complaint, the monk carefully
retraced his steps. But halfway across the stream, he
made a sudden move to throw Robin off his back.

Robin gripped hard with his arms and legs. "Not
quite yet, my friend," he said. "I prefer to reach the
bank with dry shoes."

"As you please," the monk laughed. As they reached
the water's edge, he suddenly dropped to one knee.
Robin flew through the air and hit the ground with a
thump. He was on his feet in time to grab the monk in
a wrestler's hold.

Robin soon realized that he had met his match as a

The monk flung Robin to the ground.

wrestler. With one skillful throw, the monk flung Robin to the ground, sat on him, and cried, "Submit?"

"I submit!" replied Robin. "For a man of the Church, you are a fearsome wrestler!"

"We men of God are required to wrestle with Satan. Wrestling with men is good practice," chuckled the monk.

As they all made their way to the monk's shack, Robin said, "So you are Friar Tuck!"

"The same," said Tuck. "And you, I am certain, are Robin Hood. I'm not sure that an outlaw is fit company for a man of peace." But he grinned slyly as he spoke and fetched mugs and a pitcher of ale.

Robin looked around. For a man of peace, Tuck was well armed. A sword hung on a wall.

"Will you join our company?" Robin asked the Friar.

"I shall think about it," Tuck replied. "It can be lonely here—except when Gisborne's men come bothering me!"

When the outlaws rose to go, Tuck rose, too. "I'll accompany you part of the way," he said.

They had gone barely a mile when Little John said, "Listen! Someone's in trouble!"

They heard shouting and the clash of weapons. They hurried toward the noise and soon came upon a crowd of men engaged in battle.

"Gisborne's cutthroats!" cried Tuck. "And my sword left hanging on the wall!" He picked up a stout tree branch and charged down the slope. The outlaws could hardly keep up with him.

One of Gisborne's men was trying to pull a white-haired man from his horse. Tuck whirled the branch around and sent the attacker spinning.

Taken by surprise, Gisborne's men were quickly overcome. Some fled, while the rest were brought down by well-aimed arrows.

"I'm in your debt," said the white-haired man. "I'm Simon of Lincoln. Those villains would have stolen the goods I was taking to Nottingham market."

One of Simon's people was badly injured. "You must rest before continuing," Robin said. "Be our guests tonight, and tomorrow we will see you safely to Nottingham."

The next morning, Simon of Lincoln prepared to leave. "I owe you a great deal, including my life," he said. "I must reward you. Most of you could use some new garments. Perhaps this will help." He presented Robin with a bolt of fine, dark green, woolen cloth. "This was woven in my own town. There we call it Lincoln green," he explained.

"Thank you, Simon," Robin replied, accepting the cloth.

Escorted by Will Scarlett, Simon and his people went on their way. When Will returned, he had news.

"Prince John is holding an archery contest," he said, "to find the champion bowman of all England. The prize is a silver arrow."

Little John frowned. "This is no ordinary contest," he observed. "Why hold it in a small town like Nottingham? I think Prince John has only one purpose—to lure Robin into a trap."

"You may be right," said Robin, "but I must take part. A Saxon victory would be a great thing for the people—and, better still, a blow to John and his Norman friends."

On the day of the contest, the outlaws made their way to Nottingham. Robin wore old, shabby clothes. His face, grimy with wood ash, was hidden by his long, hooded cloak. His hair and beard were uncombed. He looked like a beggar.

Stands had been erected, and the targets were set up on the common land outside the town. Vendors in busy stalls sold food and drink. Flags fluttered in the breeze over the colorful pavilions of the nobility. Over the largest tent flew the standard of the crafty Prince John.

Amid the splendor, people crowded from far and

near, eager to see who the winner would be. Soldiers of the garrison kept a close watch on the crowd. But the outlaws came in ones and twos, keeping their weapons hidden under their cloaks. They blended in with the townspeople. Robin entered the competition grounds alone and reported to the marshals by himself.

At last the contest began. There were over eighty contestants. As the afternoon passed, they were gradually eliminated, until only four were left. Robin was one of them. The targets were removed, and new ones were made ready.

Little John was watching anxiously, when he felt a tug at his sleeve.

It was Master Simon, the merchant. "You must get away, all of you!" he exclaimed. "Gisborne has a troop of mounted men hidden behind the royal pavilion. They will attack you as soon as you try to leave."

Little John looked around for the others. But he could not see them in the crowd, and the final round of the contest was about to begin.

"That is our man," the prince declared.

The targets were slender willow branches, set upright in the ground. An arrow that did not strike true would glance off the slippery wood and not count as a hit.

In the royal pavilion, Prince John and the Sheriff of Nottingham watched the competitors closely, looking for clues. One of the archers had to be Robin Hood! Suddenly, the prince spoke up.

"That is our man," he declared, pointing.

"Do you mean the beggar, Your Highness?" asked the sheriff.

"No beggar stands so proud in front of his betters," answered the prince. "If that is not Robin Hood, then I am not John Lackland!"

The first archer prepared to shoot. Thinking quickly, Little John leaned down and whispered to one of his Saxon neighbors, "They say the tall one is Robin Hood!"

The Saxon whispered excitedly to others around him, and soon the whispers ran all through the crowd:

47

"Robin Hood? Is it? Yes, surely! It is! It's Robin Hood!"

There was a hush as the first archer loosed an arrow. He missed. So did the second man. There was a gasp as the third archer's arrow grazed the willow branch, but then it, too, hit the ground.

Now it was the hooded man's turn. He carefully took aim, then fired. A great roar of applause went up from the crowd. His arrow split the willow cleanly.

Prince John stood up. "Step forward, archer!" he cried. "Champion bowman of all England...by a lucky shot!"

"Lucky!" cried Robin. In one smooth movement he turned and shot another arrow. It hit the first squarely and split it neatly in two.

The prince sneered. "I knew you would be unable to resist...Robin Hood!"

"Guards!" shouted the Sheriff. "Arrest him!"

But his voice was lost in the crowd's roar. The cheering mob of Saxons shoved the guards aside. Warned by Little John of Gisborne's trap, the outlaws pushed their way through to Robin. As the crowd spilled out from the archery grounds, the outlaws were swept along in the confusion.

Tents collapsed and booths were overturned. Gisborne watched in anger as his carefully planned ambush was ruined. His soldiers tried to force their way through the mob, but their horses, startled by the uproar, plunged and reared uncontrollably. Saxons began hurling pieces of the wrecked booths at them. Finally, the horsemen were forced to retreat.

As the outlaws raced for the forest, they could hear the hoofbeats of six horses, led by Guy of Gisborne, rapidly closing in on them.

Robin, Little John, Mutch, and Nic formed a rear guard while the others sprinted for cover. Arrows whizzed all around them. Suddenly Little John went down, wounded in the leg. Mutch ran to his aid, just managing to drag him toward the trees. They were pursued by a single horseman.

Robin raised his bow and shot; the arrow missed,

It was Guy of Gisborne!

but the horseman fell down from his steed and lay silent, stunned. It was Guy of Gisborne!

"You missed him!" cried Gilbert in disbelief.

"When the time comes, Guy of Gisborne and Robin of Locksley will meet in combat face to face," said Robin. "But now, I still have some unfinished business with Prince John."

"Prince John?" asked Will Scarlett.

"Yes," said Robin, grinning. "He forgot to present me with my silver arrow!"

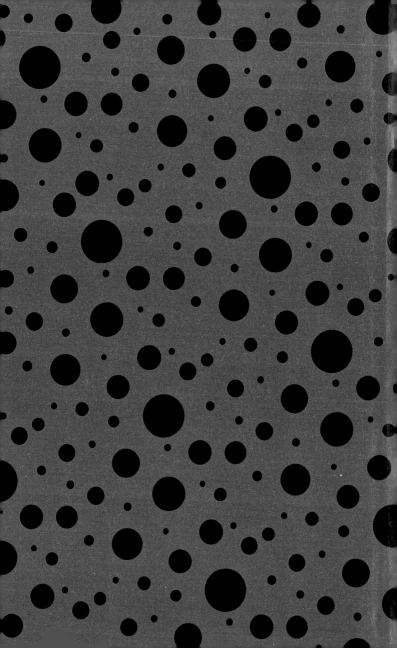